A Note to Parents and Caregivers:

Read-it! Readers are for children who are just starting on the amazing road to reading. These beautiful books support both the acquisition of reading skills and the love of books.

 The PURPLE LEVEL presents basic topics and objects using high frequency words and simple language patterns.

 The RED LEVEL presents familiar topics using common words and repeating sentence patterns.

 The BLUE LEVEL presents new ideas using a larger vocabulary and varied sentence structure.

 The YELLOW LEVEL presents more challenging ideas, a broad vocabulary, and wide variety in sentence structure.

 The GREEN LEVEL presents more complex ideas, an extended vocabulary range, and expanded language structures.

 The ORANGE LEVEL presents a wide range of ideas and concepts using challenging vocabulary and complex language structures.

When sharing a book with your child, read in short stretches, pausing often to talk about the pictures. Have your child turn the pages and point to the pictures and familiar words. And be sure to reread favorite stories or parts of stories.

There is no right or wrong way to share books with children. Find time to read with your child, and pass on the legacy of literacy.

Adria F. Klein, Ph.D.
Professor Emeritus
California State University
San Bernardino, California

First American edition published in 2005 by
Picture Window Books
5115 Excelsior Boulevard
Suite 232
Minneapolis, MN 55416
877-845-8392
www.picturewindowbooks.com

First published in Canada in 1999 by
Les éditions Héritage inc.
300 Arran Street, Saint Lambert
Quebec, Canada J4R 1K5

Library of Congress Cataloging-in-Publication Data
Grampy's bad day / author: Dominique Demers ; illustrator: Daniel Dumont.
p. cm. — (Read-it! readers)
Summary: To cheer up his grandson, a grandfather recounts the story of a very bad day
he once had.
ISBN 1-4048-1073-0 (hardcover)
[1. Grandfathers—Fiction.] I. Dumont, Daniel, ill. II. Title. III. Series.

PZ7.D3919Gr 2005
[E]—dc22
2004024890

Grampy's Bad Day

Written by Dominique Demers
Illustrated by Daniel Dumont

Special thanks to our advisers for their expertise:

Adria F. Klein, Ph.D.
Professor Emeritus, California State University
San Bernardino, California

Susan Kesselring, M.A.
Literacy Educator
Rosemount - Apple Valley - Eagan (Minnesota) School District

PICTURE WINDOW BOOKS
Minneapolis, Minnesota

My name is Paul. That's my name because my father's name is Paul and my godfather's name is Paul. I am nine years old.

I am pretty good in school, but I am super good on a skateboard, a snowboard, roller skates, and at snowball fights.

This is my grandfather and my best friend. He is eighty years old—almost ten times my age! His real name is Herman, but I always call him Grampy.

My grandmother's name is Mamie. She says Grandpa is a bad cook. She also says he is an old rascal, a good husband, and one great storyteller! That is very true.

When I am bored after school or on a Saturday, I often go to Grampy's house. Time goes so fast with him. He tells stories about the old times, when he was a kid.

8

It's a little hard to imagine because Grampy is so old, but before being a grandfather, Grampy was a little boy—just like me!

Last time Grampy and I were together, I was in a really bad mood. A boy named Mark had told everyone that I liked Samantha. Not true! Everything but true! Mark is an awful liar.

As revenge, I called him an ugly slug. The whole thing ended—in the principal's office.

I asked Grampy if he ever went through such an awful day when he was young. Grampy didn't answer right away. He did what he always does when I ask him a question: he scratched his chin, looked at the ceiling, and twisted the long hairs that come out of his ears. Then, and only then, did he answer me.

"When I was your age, young man, I went through the worst day of my life. I remember it as if it were yesterday. Back then, I was in love with a girl," Grampy said.

"You, Grampy? In love with a girl?" I asked.

"Well yes! I was madly in love with a girl with red hair. I saw her everywhere—even in my soup!" Grampy said.

I looked at Grampy and asked him, "You saw her even in your soup?"

"I was thinking about her all the time! I imagined holding hands with her. I dreamed about giving her a little kiss on the cheek," Grampy said.

"You Grampy? You would have done that?"
I asked.

"I was thinking about it anyway—that day
was her birthday, and I had decided to give
her the nicest gift of all," Grampy said.

18

"The nicest gift of all? It had to be a skateboard!" I said.

"No, no, Paul! Skateboards had not been invented yet. I had earned twenty-five cents by collecting bottle caps—a small fortune at the time! Twenty-five cents to buy my love a bag of candies like she had never seen. Black pipes." Grampy said.

"Black pipes, how come?" I asked.

"Not real pipes—little black licorice pipes with red sugar at the tip,"Grampy said.

"Oh," I said.

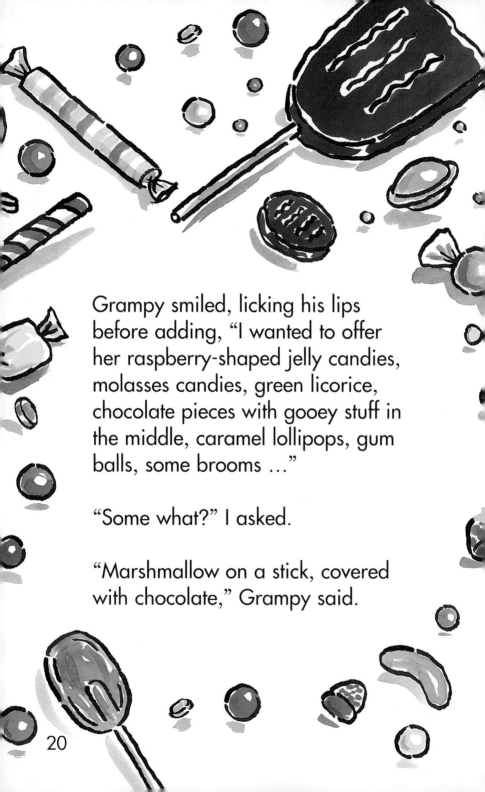

Grampy smiled, licking his lips before adding, "I wanted to offer her raspberry-shaped jelly candies, molasses candies, green licorice, chocolate pieces with gooey stuff in the middle, caramel lollipops, gum balls, some brooms ..."

"Some what?" I asked.

"Marshmallow on a stick, covered with chocolate," Grampy said.

"Yum!" I yelled.

"But on that day, EVERYTHING went wrong.
First, I woke up with a horrible toothache,"
Grampy said.

"Maybe because you liked candies
so much!" I said.

Grampy shrugged his shoulders and continued, "Anyway, my mother had given me fifty cents to go to the tooth puller."

"The tooth puller?" I asked.

"Oh yes. Back in my time, we didn't go to the dentist. Twenty-five cents was all it took to have a tooth pulled out. And believe me, it hurt, but for another twenty-five cents he would give us medicine so it wouldn't hurt so much," Grampy said.

"On that morning, I went to school with seventy-five cents: twenty-five cents to pull the tooth out, twenty-five cents for the pain medicine, and twenty-five cents to buy the candies. I felt like a real millionaire!"

I laughed at my grandfather. I said, "Grampy, you're exaggerating!"

At the same time, Grandma yelled, "Herman, you're exaggerating!"

"Anyways, while walking to school, I got into a fight with John Ives. We rolled on the gravel, and I lost one of my quarters. I didn't have enough money for the candy. I was desperate! Just then I got an idea—a terrible idea!" Grampy said.

"Oh no! Grampy! I think I know! You didn't do it, did you?" I asked.

"Oh yes! I gave only twenty-five cents to the tooth puller, and I suffered horribly," Grampy said.

Right then, my Grandma came out of the kitchen with her hands on her hips. She said, "Herman, you are exaggerating again!"

"I almost fainted," argued Grampy, "but it was worth it because I was in love!"

"Poor Grampy! Did you, at least, give the candy to the pretty girl? Did you hold hands with her? And give her a little kiss on the cheek?" I asked.

"What do you think?" replied Grampy, "I told you, it was the WORST day of my life. I bought the candy and went looking for my pretty redhead. I found her in the woods near her house—with John Ives. I saw him holding her hand, and he even gave her a little kiss on the cheek!

"On no! And what did you do?" I asked.

"I went back home and, don't tell anyone, I cried. I couldn't even eat the candy because my mouth hurt so much." Grampy said.

"Poor Grampy! I think that day was even worse than mine. That's not the end of the story I hope. It would be too awful!" I said.

"Oh yes! That's the way it ended. But do you know what happened to the redheaded girl fifteen years later?" Grampy said.

"Fifteen years later? Well, no. What?" I asked.

"Well, I married her!" Grampy exclaimed.

"What? It was Grandma?" I asked.

"Of course! She had long red hair back then. And she was a cutie!" Grampy said.

With a grin, Grandma said, "Herman, you're always exaggerating!"

More *Read-it!* Readers

Bright pictures and fun stories help you practice your reading skills. Look for more books at your level.

A Clown in Love by Mireille Villeneuve
Alex and the Game of the Century by Gilles Tibo
Alex and Toolie by Gilles Tibo
Daddy's an Alien by Bruno St-Aubin
Emily Lee Carole Temblay
Forrest and Freddy by Gilles Tibo
Gabby's School by the Sea by Marie-Danielle Croteau
Grampy's Bad Day by Dominique Demers
John's Day by Marie-Francine Hébert
Lulu and the Magic Box by Lucie Papineau
Peppy, Patch, and the Postman by Marisol Sarrazin
Peppy, Patch, and the Socks by Marisol Sarrazin
The Princess and the Frog by Margaret Nash
Rachel's Adventure Ring by Sylvia Roberge Blanchet
Run! by Sue Ferraby
Sausages! by Anne Adeney
Stickers, Shells, and Snow Globes by Dana Meachen Rau
Theodore the Millipede by Carole Tremblay
The Truth About Hansel and Gretel by Karina Law
When Nobody's Looking... by Louise Tondreau-Levert

Looking for a specific title or level? A complete list of *Read-it!* Readers is available on our Web site: *www.picturewindowbooks.com*